TROUBLE'S CHILD

Also from Terry Goodkind
Nest
The Girl in the Moon
Crazy Wanda

TROUBLE'S CHILD

AN ANGELA CONSTANTINE NOVELLA

TERRY GOODKIND

Skyhorse Publishing
NEW YORK

Skyhorse Publishing books may be purchased in bulk at special discounts for sales promotion, corporate gifts, fund-raising, or educational purposes. Special editions can also be created to specifications. For details, contact the Special Sales Department, Skyhorse Publishing, 307 West 36th Street, 11th Floor, New York, NY 10018 or info@skyhorsepublishing.com.

Skyhorse® and Skyhorse Publishing® are registered trademarks of Skyhorse Publishing, Inc.®, a Delaware corporation.

Visit our website at www.skyhorsepublishing.com.

10 9 8 7 6 5 4 3 2 1

Library of Congress Cataloging-in-Publication Data is available on file.

Print-on-Demand Paperback ISBN: 978-1-5107-4802-6
Ebook ISBN: 978-1-5107-3980-2

Cover design by Rob Anderson

ONE

Angela slowly reached under her coat for her gun as she carefully reversed her steps to back away from the corpse of a young woman.

She forced herself not to make any sudden moves, and especially not to run. She gripped the weapon in both hands, locking her aim between the piercing eyes of the predator guarding its meal.

She stole a quick glance around at the silent, snowy woods, looking for any other threat. She saw none, but she knew that in the fading gray light the woods could easily conceal someone, or something, lurking behind expanses of brush and young fir trees.

Although the creature hunched over the corpse looked like it might be a cross between a wolf and a German shepherd, this was not someone's pet.

There was a hint of coloration beneath the mostly black fur. Its winter coat had long since come in, giving it a thick ruff. Against the white snow it was an intimidating sight.

Angela knew that wolves sometimes made their way down from Canada. She could only assume that along the way a female must have bred with a big shepherd. There was no doubt in her mind that the resulting wolf dog snarling at her was as dangerous as it was powerful.

She checked the surrounding woods for others. This animal appeared to be alone. If there were a pack, she would have seen some of them. They would have wanted in on the meal.

Pack or not, this wolf's bared fangs told her that it was more than willing to fight to keep its scavenged meal. Or make a meal of her.

There were ligature bruises and lacerations on the dead woman's neck, so Angela knew that the wolf hadn't been the one that had killed her. She had been murdered. Angry, red, human bite wounds on the breasts told her this was a killing out of hate and rage. Whoever had done this had likely killed before. Angela knew that this kind of killer would kill again if not stopped.

She was often amazed that she had never ended up like the dead woman. It could easily have happened to her more times than she cared to remember. That gave her a unique empathy with these kinds of victims—women who had not been lucky enough to survive. It also gave her a purpose in life.

The light, fluffy snow had only just begun to cover the ground and trees, gradually turning the forest white, but that snow had only started to accumulate on the hands stretched out over the dead woman's head. There was still enough warmth in the body to melt the big flakes. This woman had not been dead long.

The wolf had both front paws protectively over the naked corpse, clearly ready to defend its meal. Its muzzle dripped blood and gore. Wisps of steam from the open belly rose into the cold, still air. Wolves were predators that hunted large hoofed mammals like elk, deer, and moose, but they were not above scavenging dead animals for a meal.

It might have been nature's way, but Angela didn't like seeing an animal tearing into the body of a freshly dead human. She understood that it wasn't a malicious act, and she certainly had no desire to kill such a magnificent creature.

She wanted to fire a round to scare the wolf off, but since the woman hadn't been dead for very long it was possible the killer was still nearby. If so, she didn't want to tip him off that she was there and give him a chance to ambush her. She didn't want to be his second kill of the day.

Angela felt a hot wave of emotion igniting at the prospect that the killer might still be nearby and that she might be able to catch him. It had been quite a while since those inner needs had been sated. Now, they were again crackling to life.

Once Angela had backed far enough away, the animal went back to ripping out bloody pieces and gobbling them down. It looked to be starving.

There were a lot of bird tracks around the body from the nearby ravens waiting for their turn at the carrion. Every once in a while one of the ravens would carefully approach the carcass, put one foot forward, then spring back when the wolf snapped at it. Ravens were opportunistic and often followed wolves to have a chance at the scraps.

Angela saw that there were also human tracks, but the snow was light and fluffy, and there wasn't yet enough of it to make for good identification of the footprints. She saw those footprints and the drag marks going off to her right, toward the highway. The snow was picking up, so she knew that what footprints there were would soon vanish beneath a growing blanket of white.

The wolf guarded its meal as Angela inspected the footprints and drag marks leading off through the trees toward the highway. The woman had apparently been dragged in by her ankles and dropped. That was why her arms were stretched out above her head.

Angela reluctantly left the animal to its meal so she could follow the drag marks, hoping she might be lucky enough to catch the man who had done this. Even with the snow beginning to accumulate, the trail was still easy enough to follow.

She was acutely aware that this was a very recent event, and not wanting to inadvertently become the next victim, she moved cautiously, quietly, keeping an eye on the woods all around and her gun at the ready.

The body had obliterated most of the footprints as it had been dragged through the leaf litter and into the woods to be dumped.

There wasn't enough snow, yet, to make the footprints clearly readable, but she could see enough to tell that the killer had followed the drag marks back to where he had come from.

By the time she reached the highway, there was no sign of the killer. She saw tire marks in the gravel where he had backed off the road a short distance into the woods so his vehicle wouldn't be easily seen by passing cars.

The tread marks weren't distinct enough to be identifiable. There were smears in the snow where the body had been thrown on the ground and then dragged off into the woods like a sack of garbage.

Angela looked up and down the empty highway, then finally relaxed a little. The killer was gone. Frustration took over at missing her chance to have him. She had been so close, and now she had no idea who he was or where he had gone.

But if she ever got the chance to look into his eyes, she would know him and know what he had done.

Angela pulled out her phone. She was too far out of Milford Falls for the police, so she expected her 911 call would go instead to the sheriff's office.

TWO

Angela looked up when she heard a car coming from off around the bend of the lonely road. The snow, along with the wind, was picking up. She saw the flashing lights on the distant wall of snow-crusted trees. Not wanting a sheriff's deputy to see that she had a gun, Angela put her Glock back in the holster at the small of her back.

She usually carried a Walther P22 in her truck, but when she went hiking for the day she carried a 9 mm Glock. The .22 was like a scalpel, with virtually no worry about overpenetration. The Glock was like a hatchet. In the woods, where she might encounter a bear, she didn't care about overpenetration, so she carried the Glock. Either way, she didn't want the police to see her with a gun.

As a rule she always did her best to avoid talking to police, but this time it was necessary. Angela didn't like the thought of the woman's remains being left out in these woods all alone for animals to feed on. She should be taken back and put to rest with respect. Since the authorities would likely never find the body on their own, Angela had to show them where it was, and to do that she had to talk to law enforcement.

When the white sheriff's car with red stripes came around the curve, lights flashing, she stepped out on the edge of the road and held up an arm so the deputy would see her. The car slowed as it pulled over, tires crunching to a stop in the snowy gravel.

The deputy put on a black Stetson hat as he unfolded himself out of his car. His uniform was black, and he wore a black leather jacket. He was tall, with creased, sunken cheeks and the kind of eyes that said everyone was guilty of something. He looked to be about twenty years older than Angela, maybe in his early to middle forties.

His steely gaze locked on her as he closed the door and strode purposefully to the front of his car.

"You the one who called us?"

"Yes." Angela pointed up into the woods. "I found the body of a dead woman up there."

Not turning to look where she pointed, he instead continued to stare at her. "And what were you doing up there?"

"It's my day off. I was going for a hike."

"A hike. In the preserve." There was nothing illegal about that, but he made it sound somehow criminal. "Day off from what?"

"I have a courier service. And I tend bar."

"Uh-huh." He regarded her as if she might be the killer. "What's your name?"

"Angela Constantine."

His gold name tag, with A. NOLAN in black letters, stood out against his black shirt. He looked professional. Hard-ass professional. And dangerous. She was already regretting having placed the call.

His glare took in her platinum-blond, red-tipped hair, the earrings down the back of her ear, finally settling on the tattoo across her throat.

"Let me see your ID."

She wanted to ask him why, but she had a rule never to argue with authorities. She wanted to always remain above suspicion and to never be regarded as trouble. She pulled her driver's license out of her pocket and handed it to him, trying to look friendly and cooperative.

He took it without a word and went back to his car to run her name through their system. In a few minutes he came back, she thought looking a little disappointed that she didn't turn up as being wanted for murder.

"Constantine," he said to himself as he stood before her carefully looking over her license. He looked up. "Your hair is blue on your license."

Angela shrugged. "I like to dye my hair different colors."

He nodded his dissatisfaction to himself as his eyes narrowed. "I know a Constantine residence—in the trailer park in Milford Falls."

"That's my mother's place," Angela volunteered before he could accuse her of living there, or of her mother's sins.

He was looking at her like he was beginning to suspect she must have drugs on her. "I've been there a few times. You had to still be living there when I pulled people with warrants out of there. Along with lots of drugs."

Angela wanted to say she didn't do drugs, but she knew that would make it sound like she did, so she kept her mouth shut.

"Nothing but lowlifes living there," he said, "doing drugs day and night. Drinking, fighting, fencing stolen goods."

He did indeed know the place. Angela had grown up in the midst of all that. Because of all the meth, heroin, and booze continually in her mother's system when she had been pregnant, Angela had been born different from other people. She knew she could never be normal. She was a freak.

"I'm sure I remember arresting your mother along with some scumbag drug dealers at that trailer."

"Probably," was all Angela said.

"Your mother is a tweaker. Every time I saw her she was flying on crystal meth."

"Yeah, well, that's why I moved out."

He idly tapped her license on the knuckles of his other hand. "Who's your father?"

"I don't have any idea," Angela said with a shrug.

He had undoubtedly been one of her mother's dealers or a random tweaker. She was always getting laid by one or the other.

The deputy's glare looked to have formed permanent creases in his brow. "Everyone in that trailer was trouble. You grew up there. Now you go for a hike, wandering around out in these vast woods, and you just happen to find a dead body."

"Yes, so I called 911."

He handed her license back to her. "Let me see your hands. Both of them. Hold them up."

Angela did as he asked, fingers spread, showing him the fronts and backs of both hands. She knew he was looking for defensive wounds. He wanted to satisfy himself that she hadn't been in a fight and killed the woman.

He grunted his dissatisfaction that her hands were clean and free of any wounds. "Your mother is trouble. That means you're the child of trouble."

Angela looked off down the road. She was just about to tell him to go find the fucking dead body on his own when he gestured toward the woods.

"Come on. Show me what you found." He put emphasis on the word "found" like he thought she had invented the story.

Without a word, Angela turned and headed into the woods. The fat flakes were falling faster. The drag marks were already mostly covered over, as were her own footprints, but she knew the way.

THREE

When they pushed balsam limbs out of their way and came out from the thick brush and trees, they saw the body off in a low area of the clearing.

"Jesus Christ!" Deputy Nolan shouted as he drew his sidearm.

The wolf, still guarding its prize, rose up, snarling and snapping.

Without hesitation Deputy Nolan fired off two quick shots. The second shot went high and just flicked the hackles on the animal's back. The wolf bolted away. At the sound of the shots the ravens all took to wing, squawking their surprise and displeasure. They scattered in all directions, disappearing into the trees.

The deputy took two steps forward and emptied his gun as fast as he could at the wolf as it raced away, kicking up snow in its wake.

"Why didn't you tell me about that damn animal feeding on the body!"

"It wasn't here before," she lied.

"Well," he growled as he pulled out the empty magazine and shoved in a full one, "that should keep the filthy beast away. I think I may have hit it."

Angela didn't mention that he had pulled down and to the right when he fired the first shot, a common mistake, so that first round hit the murder victim in the rib cage.

Deputy Nolan racked the slide to chamber a round and then holstered the weapon before approaching the corpse. He looked around carefully for tracks. Any that had been there were now covered with snow. His circle got smaller as he closed in on the dead woman. He finally knelt down beside the corpse and pointed at the neck.

"See here? Looks like she's been strangled."

Angela wanted to say "No shit," but she kept her mouth shut. She couldn't imagine the horror of being strangled to death like that, the terror of not being able to breathe.

Deputy Nolan looked at the many human bite wounds on the breasts but didn't mention them.

"Looks like maybe her ribs have been broken," he said as he looked more closely at the marks on her side.

Angela pointed. "Your first shot hit her in the ribs."

He cast her a sour look but didn't say anything.

He finally stood and made a call on his radio. He reported what he had found and asked for a crime scene team and the coroner.

Despite not liking having to deal with law enforcement, Angela felt better that someone would finally take proper care of the woman's body.

When the deputy finished on the radio he turned his attention back to Angela.

"Did you see anyone or anything out of the ordinary—other than this body?"

Angela shook her head. "No, nothing."

He looked down to study the woman's face for a moment. "Do you know her?"

Angela had seen the woman in the bar a few times, but not enough to know her name. "I'm afraid not."

He shook his head once. "She's a prostitute."

Angela wasn't surprised. "How do you know that?"

"Her name is Kristi something." He considered a moment. "Kristi Green, I think. She's been arrested for soliciting a number of times. I remember the face. She hung out in the area of the Riley Motel. Whores use the Riley to conduct their business."

Angela tended bar down the hill from the Riley, so she knew all about it. The prostitutes who used the motel didn't waste their time coming down to socialize with customers at Barry's Place, the bar where she worked. Occasionally, though, they would hang out there hoping to pick up a customer. Most of them used the Internet now, rather than invite trouble from police by soliciting in bars or hotels.

"I showed you where I found her. I don't know anything else," Angela said. "If it's okay with you I'd like to get home before it gets too dark. And I'm getting awfully cold just standing around," she added, trying to elicit some human sympathy from the man.

He appraised her with a look lacking human sympathy. "Where do you live?"

Angela pointed. "I have a place over that way. Next to the preserve."

"If you wait·until help arrives and this business here gets taken care of, I can give you a ride."

"Well . . ." Angela drawled as if she were actually considering it. The last thing in the world she wanted to do was get in a cop car with this hard-ass and have him come to her house. "It's not that long of a walk. I'd like to get home."

Actually, it was a rather long walk, and it would be dark soon, so she would have to hurry to make it home before it was too dark to see.

"Yeah, sure," he said with a flick of his hand. "Go ahead. I need to go back to my car and start writing this up while I wait. I have your information from your license so if we need anything else we'll know how to get in touch with you." He opened his wallet. "If you think of anything else we should know, give me a call. Here's my card."

The card had "Deputy A. Nolan" printed to the left of a sheriff's badge. There was a phone number below his name. The phone number was one of those repeated numbers that stuck in her head.

Sometimes numbers did that and she couldn't get rid of them. She knew she would never have any reason to call him.

"Okay, if I think of anything else I'll call you," Angela said as she slipped the card into the pocket with her driver's license. "Do you mind me asking your first name?"

His glare was back. "Not at all. It's Deputy."

All right, then, she thought. *Asshole it is.*

FOUR

Because she had spent so much time waiting for the deputy and then with him and the dead woman, it was getting much later in the day than she would have liked. The light was seriously gloomy, to say nothing of the increasing snow.

If it got dark on her, Angela wanted to be on a road rather than in the pitch-black woods. She carried a small flashlight, but still, in the woods it would be slow slogging and dangerous.

She knew that if she went down to the road where Deputy Nolan's car was parked and walked home from there, it was quite a distance, because the road first wound around a mountain to the south before coming back up north and then past her place. By taking a shortcut over the ridge she would get to that same road, but after it went on that loop for miles out of the way. Going through the woods over the ridge saved miles of walking.

As she plodded up the hill, head down against the snow swirling around fir trees and blowing in her face, she spotted tracks. They went in the same direction as she was headed. After following them for a time, and because they were so clear in the fresh snow, she realized they had to be the tracks left by the wolf when it ran away as Deputy Nolan shot at it.

When her foot displaced some of the fresh snow, she saw blood beneath the top layer of white. The wolf had apparently been hit by at least one of the deputy's bullets.

The farther Angela went, the closer she knew she was getting to the wolf. It was becoming clear to her that the wounded animal was bleeding and slowing down. She drew her gun and kept it out as she crossed the ridge. She didn't want to come on an injured wolf and be defenseless if it attacked.

As she reached the bottom of the far side of the ridge, not far from the highway, she came upon the wounded animal. It lay on its side in the snow, panting in distress. There was a good amount of blood in the snow.

Her first thought was to put the animal out of its misery. It was clearly suffering and would not survive. She stood back and pointed her gun down at its head. One eye rolled back, watching her. She stood over it, looking into that eye. She hated to shoot the animal, but she didn't want it to die a long, painful death, either.

It occurred to her, then, that if she shot the wolf, Deputy Nolan, just back over the ridge, would hear the shot. He would come to investigate. Then she would be caught carrying a concealed weapon. Even if he let it pass, which she seriously doubted, she would have made herself noteworthy. That was something she always avoided. She didn't want that to change now, just to put this creature out of its misery.

Carefully, experimentally, she squatted down while still holding the gun pointed at the animal, and slowly reached out.

The wolf didn't move. It lay panting, watching her as she ever so slowly put a hand to its heaving chest and gently stroked the fur.

She expected a protest of some sort, even an attack, but there was nothing. It was as if the animal watching her was saying, *I'm finished. Go ahead and do what you will. I don't have it in me to stop you.*

She found herself mesmerized by stroking the warm black fur.

"I'm sorry you were hurt," she whispered to it. "I didn't mean for that to happen."

The big dark eye continued to watch her, but the wolf made no move to defend itself.

"I suppose it's my fault. I'm the one who called the police. I'm so sorry that jerk hurt you."

As she was stroking the black fur, the wolf let out a sigh, as if comforted at least a little by Angela's gentle touch and soft words.

She let out a sigh of her own. "What am I going to do now? I can't leave you here to suffer."

Listening to her voice seemed to reduce the panting.

Angela slowly stood, trying not to alarm the creature.

"I'll tell you what. I'm going to go home and get my truck. If you will let me, I'll take you to a vet and get you some help. All right? Will you let me help you?"

In answer, the wolf let out a soft whimper.

Angela knew better than to ascribe human reactions or understanding to animals, especially wild animals, but in this case she was willing to take it for a yes.

FIVE

Angela held her coat closed and the lamb's wool collar tight against her neck and ears as she hurried along just beside the shallow ditch. The road would eventually run past her place, so she knew she wouldn't get lost. Since traffic was rare on the remote road, she didn't worry too much about covering her ears and not hearing a car. There was no hunting or logging allowed in the vast preserve surrounding her place, leaving little reason for anyone to use the road or be out there unless they were taking a back way to or from the small village of Bradley.

She supposed that was one reason the killer had used the desolate area to murder Kristi Green and dump her body out here. It wasn't the first time a body had been dumped in the woods around Milford Falls and it wouldn't be the last.

Angela was a bit surprised when she saw the lights of a car coming from behind. As it drove past and its lights reflected off the snow-covered road and trees, she saw that it looked like a Lincoln that was several decades old.

The old, boxy car slowed to a stop. As it began backing up, Angela put her right hand under her coat and gripped the handle of her Glock. She could see that the car was a light tan color with a darker tan vinyl roof. The rocker panels beneath the doors, along with the lower part of the fender behind the rear wheel, had been eaten away by rust.

As the car slowly backed up it stayed toward the center of the road, rather than backing close to her. The brakes squealed as the old car rocked to a stop. Angela gripped the gun tighter, but didn't draw it. If this was a guy getting a bad idea at seeing a woman all alone on a lonely road, he would soon discover just how bad the idea really was.

The passenger door creaked and popped in protest as it opened. When it did, the interior lights came on and she could see there were two people inside.

The driver was a frumpy woman with a head of thin, frizzy hair. She had on a collarless pale blue dress with little flowers all over it. It was the kind of dress that looked like it had been found at the bottom of a box in a thrift store. Because the dome light was behind her, her face was in shadow.

The passenger was a middle-aged man in a dark suit, black shirt buttoned all the way up, and no tie. Both his hands were resting over the head of a white cane standing up between his knees. He was wearing dark glasses. It was already dark out.

Angela realized by the dark glasses, the white cane, and the way the man's head moved to hear sounds rather than look toward their source that the man was blind.

He smiled as he leaned out a little into the snowy night. When he did, she could see that in front of long sideburns he had a large cross tattooed on each cheek. His full head of straight black hair had been slicked back with a comb through styling gel.

"It's an awful night to be out in the weather," he called out into the snowy night. He was looking off at nothing, the way a blind person would, not knowing exactly where she was.

"I'm fine," Angela called back. "I'm enjoying the first snow of the season."

"It came up pretty quick. Maybe quicker than you expected? May my sister and I give you a lift to someplace warm and safe?"

Angela stood in the swirling snow, wishing this car would leave. She at least felt better knowing that she was armed.

Being the daughter of a meth addict, she knew she was a freak. She was a girl born broken. That was the reason she rarely felt anything, rarely cared about anything, but when she looked back over her shoulder she felt a pang of empathy for the wolf lying wounded in the snow.

It was an innocent victim, much like the dead woman. Now, it was suffering. The longer it took her to get back to the animal and then get it to help, the less its chances of survival would be.

"If you don't mind, I guess I could use a lift."

The man reached out with his cane and tapped the tip on the back door. "Come on, then. Get in."

Angela slammed the heavy door behind her as she climbed into the overly soft backseat. The inside of the car smelled musty, but the warmth felt good on her throbbing cold face.

"I'm Reverend Clay Baker," he said, turning his head only a little without looking back at her as the car started forward. "This is my sister Lucy."

"I'm Angela. Thanks for the lift. My house is up the road a few miles, on the right. You can drop me there."

"What are you doing on foot so far from home at night, in a snowstorm no less?" he asked.

"I have a day off, so I went for a hike through the woods. I . . . got distracted off the path and didn't realize how late it was or how far I was from home. But the road leads back home so I knew I couldn't get lost."

"Ah," he said with a nod. "A lot of young people get distracted these days and stray off the path." He chuckled at his own double entendre.

Lucy, hands at ten and two on the big, thin-rimmed steering wheel, stared ahead as she drove into the heavy snow. Lucy struck Angela as a timid, apprehensive woman. She seemed more than a little cautious about driving in the snow. Angela wished she would hurry it up.

"What is it you do for a living, Angela, if I may ask?"

"I have a courier service and I also tend bar."

"Ah," he said again. "We are couriers, too, of a sort."

Angela frowned. "What do you mean?"

"We are a traveling ministry. We were just in Bradley for the day, but we have been staying at the Riley Motel in Milford Falls for the last month or so. Milford Falls is a much bigger place with a larger need."

The Riley Motel, just up the hill from where Angela tended bar, was a dump used by the hour by hookers and by transients who stayed by the week.

"You mean you don't preach at a church?" she asked.

"We bring the word of God to those who otherwise might not have the chance to hear it. Churches are limiting. We bring God out to those places where the people are."

Angela already wanted out of the car. "You are both ministers, then?"

"I am the minister," he said. He laid a hand on his sister's shoulder as she stared ahead into the snow, wheeling the big Lincoln down the narrow, winding road. "Lucy is the sighted one. She used to work in a hospital, but after I lost my sight in an accident, she has devoted her life to helping me in our calling."

He had a Southern accent mixed with an evangelist's practiced tone. But it was the big black cross tattooed on each cheek that really made him distinctive. That was true commitment.

Angela had a large, distinctive tattoo across her throat. She knew a thing or two about true commitment.

As she watched the dark forest gliding past to each side, she cast about for something to say into the dragging silence. "Lucy, it must be interesting watching your brother in his work."

Reverend Baker lifted his left hand out, palm up. Lucy put her fist in his cupped hand and started making a series of rapid movements. Angela immediately realized that it was some kind of sign language.

She was trying to figure out their odd relationship when he said, "Lucy is a mute. She hears, but can't speak. I am her voice. She is my eyes. Lucy lost her voice to cancer of the vocal cords. Now she is able to speak to me through our hands. She says in answer to your question that it is a blessing for her to be at my side and see the chosen welcomed into God's embrace."

"That's nice that you have each other."

Reverend Baker nodded as he stared off into his blank vision. "Yes, it is a blessing. I believe that God wants us together in our calling and so He afflicted us each in ways that meant we could only accomplish His work if we work together."

Angela realized that since he couldn't see, Lucy couldn't use conventional sign language. He wouldn't be able to see her signing, so she used the odd language of letters or words signed into his hand.

"Do you know God, child?" he asked in a thin, rising tone without looking back from the front seat.

"I've met the devil on a few occasions."

Being a freak of nature from all the drugs her mother took, Angela had been born with the strange ability to recognize killers and know what they had done by looking into their eyes.

He chuckled at her answer and was apparently so taken by it that he didn't press the issue.

In the snowy light from the headlights, Angela at last spotted her driveway. She hurriedly leaned against the front seats and pointed forward between them.

"There. That's my drive up there on the right. You can let me out there, please."

Lucy rolled the big Lincoln to a stop in front of the cable stretched across Angela's drive.

"We can drive you up to your house," Reverend Baker offered.

Angela wanted out of the car and away from these two, and she certainly didn't have time to have them come up to her house and preach the gospel to her.

"Thanks, but it's not necessary." She popped open the door. "I can walk up to my place before I would get the cable unlocked."

He turned enough for her to see the big black cross tattoo on his cheek. "You watch out for the devil now, will you?"

He had no idea.

"I always do. Thanks again for the ride."

SIX

Angela slowed and parked her truck at the edge of the road. She would still have to hike quite a ways through the woods to get to the injured wolf. She felt a sense of urgency and wondered if she was being foolish going to all this trouble for a wild animal that would probably die anyway.

With the heavy cloud cover there was no moon or stars, so that once she switched off the engine and killed the headlights the world became an oppressive void of total blackness. It felt a little frightening.

Once she had locked her truck, Angela switched on the light on the headband she wore over a knit hat. The headlamp would allow her to have her hands free. If for some reason the light on the headband failed, or she fell and broke it, being all alone in the woods at night in total darkness in a snowstorm could easily be fatal, so she had a backup flashlight in her pocket as well as a small light on her key chain.

Without hesitating she plunged into the woods. She had hiked these woods since she had been a little girl, but that would be of no value in the dark. The falling snow lit by the light on the headband was disorienting, but at least the light allowed her to see well enough not to walk into a tree.

The cold air felt brittle. Every time she exhaled it made a cloud around her face. Even though her footprints from earlier had been covered over, they left depressions in the fresh snow that she was able to follow.

Slogging through the snow was tiring, but those footprints from earlier led her right back to the wolf.

She was relieved to see that the animal was still alive. She could see by the marks in the snow that it had tried to get up, but in the end it had fallen back onto its right side, the way she had left it there earlier.

Angela spotted ravens up in the tree branches, patiently waiting for their meal to expire.

Patches of snow had started to collect on the wolf's fur. If it died, the carcass would quickly freeze and drift over. She wanted to try to keep that from happening.

"Okay, here's the deal," she said as she slowly squatted down, gun in one hand. "I want to help you, and I think I can, but you're going to have to let me help you."

He followed her movements with the one eye that faced up. The other was on the underside of his head, in the snow.

"If you attack me, I will kill you." She waggled the gun where he could see it. "I mean it. You try to bite me and I will shoot you in the head."

She didn't really believe he could understand a word she was saying, but she hoped the sound of her voice would be enough to calm him. She tried to make every movement slow and deliberate, the tone of every word nonthreatening.

She carefully reached out to stroke his fur the way she had earlier. Now, she could feel him trembling. That really hurt her heart. With him unable to move, the cold was settling in on him.

She pulled the blanket down off her shoulder and held it up before the animal. "See what I brought? You're too heavy for me to carry, so what I want to do is get you onto the blanket and then drag you across the snow to my truck. I think the blanket will make it pretty easy to slide you across the snow. Plastic would slide better, but I think that might stress you too much. I think you'd rather lay on a soft blanket. Am I right?"

Angela gently stroked the animal's fur as she talked to him, hoping to get across the idea that she meant him no harm, that she was going to try to help him.

His mouth was open as he panted, and she saw that he had awfully big teeth. She was acutely aware that she was very close to a very dangerous animal. She didn't want him using those teeth on her. She would hate to have to shoot him, but if he attacked her, she would not hesitate.

"Okay, what do you say we get this show on the road?"

She laid the blanket out behind the wolf's back, then gently started pushing some of it into the snow and under him. That alarmed him enough that he suddenly started scrambling to try to get up. Angela jumped back. The wolf struggled briefly, his legs wobbling, then collapsed back down onto his side.

Amazingly enough, though, he fell mostly on the blanket.

The wolf's eyes half closed as he panted.

The effort of trying to get up seemed to have used up what little fight the animal had left. He didn't protest as Angela gathered up the corners of the blanket. When she pulled it all tight, the wolf was snugly encased inside. She thought that the darkness and being cocooned in the blanket, along with not being able to see what was happening, might help to keep him calm.

Without delay, she started dragging the wolf through the woods, weaving her way among the trees, following her own tracks back to her truck. It wasn't as easy as she had imagined it would be. The weight of the animal made him sink down in the fluffy snow, rather than glide over the top of it. Still, it was the only way she was going to get him out of the woods and to help, so she held the corners of the blanket over the front of her shoulder and leaned into the weight, dragging it behind her.

The wolf didn't make any sound of protest. She thought he must be so exhausted and cold that he had given up. She knew what it felt like to be at that point of giving up.

She panted herself with the effort of pulling the heavy load through the woods. Every so often she had to tug fallen branches out of the way from under the blanket.

Several times she fell forward into the snow. Each time she got back up as quickly as possible, brushed snow off her face, and kept going. Her nose was running, and even though she had gloves on, her fingers were freezing. Her toes hurt from the cold. She ignored the discomfort of the struggle and forged onward. She kept telling herself that it wasn't all that far and she could make better time if she quit worrying about herself and only worried about getting the wounded animal to help.

When she finally reached her truck, she dropped the tailgate and sat on it briefly to catch her breath. The metal tailgate was icy cold, so she didn't sit on it for long.

She knew the hardest part would be lifting the wolf up into the bed of the truck. It had to weigh somewhere in the neighborhood of a hundred pounds.

Urged on when she heard a pitiful sound from in the blanket, she bent down and pulled the blanket back to take a look. His eyes were closed.

Angela covered him again and scooped him up in her arms, putting one arm under the front of his chest and her other arm under his rump, folding all four legs into the middle so that his weight was in the crook of her arms.

She didn't know how she did it, but with a last, mighty effort she managed to lift him up onto the tailgate. From there the blanket slid easily into the bed of the truck.

Angela gently rubbed the wolf's side as she caught her breath.

SEVEN

The warm cab of her truck finally thawed her fingers. Her thighs burned from the effort and from the icy cold. Angela pulled her gloves off with her teeth as she raced into town. She wished she could give some of the warmth inside the cab to the injured animal. She was sure that the wind blowing over him was not helping. At least he was covered with the blanket. Since she couldn't do anything about it, she did her best to hurry.

It was quite a ways into Milford Falls, but once she reached town the streets were virtually empty. Since there was no traffic, she did four-wheel drifts around corners and through red lights, not wanting to slow any more than absolutely necessary.

Angela felt a sense of triumph to finally turn in to the twenty-four-hour emergency veterinary hospital. She spun a one-eighty through the empty parking lot, stopping with the back end of her truck facing the front door.

Angela had done courier work for the emergency animal hospital several times, but she didn't really know anyone there the way she did at the regular hospital. Inside, an older woman at a computer behind the long counter asked how she could help. Angela told her that she had an injured dog and she would need help getting it inside. The receptionist called people in the back.

In a few minutes a vet tech came out through a swinging door pulling a cart behind her. She wore blue scrubs like the nurses at the hospital. She didn't look much older than Angela.

"Hi, I'm Carol. You have a dog you need help with?"

Angela gestured toward the door. "Yes. He's in my pickup. I think he may have been shot. I can't carry him by myself."

Outside she helped Angela lift the wolf, still in the blanket, onto the cart. Blood spread through the blanket and then the paper covering the stainless-steel top of the cart.

On the way in through the doors, Angela put her hand on the wolf and felt that he was still breathing.

"I'll take it from here," Carol said, rushing for the swinging door. "You can wait out here. After the doctor evaluates your dog she'll come out and talk to you."

Angela grabbed her sleeve. "Listen, Carol, you all need be careful. This dog is part wolf. It's injured and afraid. I don't want anyone to get hurt."

The woman lifted the blanket for a look. "I understand. We deal with situations like this all the time."

Angela didn't think they really did.

"I mean it. He could really hurt you."

The vet tech smiled her understanding before she started wheeling the bloody, blanket-wrapped wolf through the swinging door into the back area. "The doctor will be out to talk to you as soon as she can," she said back over her shoulder.

Angela wondered what she had gotten herself into.

"Could you fill out the admittance form, please?" the woman behind the long counter asked.

Angela took the clipboard with a pen attached by a string and sat down in one of the orange, molded plastic chairs. The form asked for all kinds of personal information. Angela never let people know where she lived. She used a box at Mike's Mail Service for her mail and packages. She put that address on the form. She filled in what other information she could. She didn't think they would have her arrested if she left a lot of blanks, so she didn't worry about it.

She was brought to a halt by the list of questions about the "pet." They wanted to know how old it was, when it last had its shots, its ailments, injuries, and all kinds of other things Angela couldn't answer. She simply wrote "found the injured dog by the side of the road" and left everything blank.

It was an hour and a half before Carol led her into a consultation room to meet with the doctor. The doctor was a big-boned woman with a warm smile and a professional disposition. She folded her arms as she leaned back against the mauve counter.

"So, is he going to be all right?" Angela asked.

The doctor peered down at Angela. "Well, that's kind of up to you."

"What do you mean?"

She regarded Angela for a moment, apparently gauging how well she could take bad news. "What's your wolf dog's name?"

Angela drew a blank. "Well, it's not exactly my pet. I live out in the country." A story she thought would be satisfactory formed in her head. "I've seen it around a few times, but I'm pretty sure it's wild. Tonight I found it laying in the ditch at the side of the road. I think some jerk must have shot it."

The doctor nodded. "I see. Well, I think you're right. We have him sedated right now so he's comfortable. What we do next is up to you." She handed Angela two pages with a lot of boxes checked and things written in. "The wolf dog is going to die if we don't do emergency surgery. It sounds like he doesn't belong to anyone, so I guess it depends on how much he means to you."

Angela looked down at the forms. The doctor leaned in to point with her pen at several items. "This is for anesthesia, the IV drip, an MRI, the operation itself, various miscellaneous things we'll need, and the estimated stay under observation."

In the rear of the building, beyond the door at the back of the consultation room, small dogs barked nonstop. One cried continually. It was nerve-racking trying to think with all the racket.

"So what's the bottom line," Angela asked. "How much?"

"It's this number here, but this is just an initial estimate. We won't know for sure until we see how much damage was done to know if it will cost more or not. And you can see here with the total, it's going to be at least thirty-four hundred dollars. I'll do my best not to go over that, but if we're going to operate we'll have to do what we have to do."

Angela wasn't surprised by the estimate. She had expected at least that much. She knew surgery wasn't cheap. When she had gone home to get her truck she had brought four thousand dollars in cash with her. She let out a deep breath. That was a lot of money for a wild animal that still might not even make it.

She had started out the day just wanting to go for a hike in the woods, to have some peace and quiet, to get away from the drunks and guys in the bar always hitting on her.

She felt a pang of guilt for thinking only about herself. That woman she found, Kristi Green, had a much worse day. She had been brutally murdered.

"Can you save him?"

The doctor was ready with an answer. "I think so. The thing is, he's hurt pretty bad so I can't promise anything. Right now we have him anesthetized—he's asleep. If you prefer we can just let him go. He's not a pet so I would certainly understand that decision. He will feel no pain, I promise. It's up to you if you want to let him go and have a peaceful, pain-free end to his life. I can make that happen."

"But you can operate and save him?"

"I can't promise, but I'm pretty damn good."

To a degree Angela felt responsible for the creature being shot. She was the one who had called the police. Then that jerk deputy showed up, shooting first and asking questions later.

It was just a wild animal. But still . . .

"Angela, I can't afford the time to describe the damage and injuries right now or what I need to do. If you want to let him go, I completely understand. But if you want me to try to save his life, time is of the essence. He's losing a lot of blood. I need to get in there and operate immediately if you want me to try to save him."

Angela didn't know why, but she didn't want his life to end this way.

"I'd like you to go ahead and do the surgery. I'd like you to do everything you can to save his life. I'll pay for it."

EIGHT

The doctor was apparently as good as she'd said she was. The wolf survived the surgery. They thought everything had gone as well as they were hoping.

Angela was relieved.

She came by the animal hospital every day to check up on him. At first it was sad seeing him lying in a small enclosure, a blanket covering him, an IV in a shaved spot on his front leg. The vet techs assured her that he was getting pain medication and he was resting comfortably. His eyes were closed and he was unresponsive to all the barking and yapping of the other dogs.

He belonged in the woods, running free.

The third day she visited the animal hospital the wolf was awake. He didn't get up, but his eyes turned to look at her when she walked up to the enclosure door, which had clear plastic on the top half. She talked softly to him for a few minutes. She wanted to reach in and stroke his fur, but she suspected that would be a bad idea. The people there had equipment to handle him. They were careful with him, and about their own safety.

On the fourth day Carol told her that he had eaten and was doing remarkably well and getting stronger all the time. The doctor said that he could go home the next day. That eventuality had been continually on Angela's mind and she didn't know what in the world she was going to do when he was released.

She obviously couldn't take him home into her house. He would likely kill her. He was beautiful and had his place in the world. But he wasn't domesticated and never could be. He was a wild animal and that was what she wanted for him—to be wild.

Fortunately, the animal hospital had an old dog crate someone had donated. The vet techs told Angela that she could have it and that they would get the wolf dog into the crate for her so she could take him home.

When Angela came the next day to pick up the wolf, they had managed to get him into the crate. He cowered in the back and snarled when anyone got close.

"He's been here long enough that we've all gotten kind of fond of the big guy," Carol said. "We rarely see wolf dogs in here. He's magnificent. We named him Bardolph. 'Bardolph' means 'ferocious.' He's shy like most wolves, but he's also pretty ferocious."

Angela thought it a fitting name.

Carol and a male orderly helped lift the crate into the bed of Angela's pickup and tie it down.

Carol handed her some papers. "These are instructions on his postoperative care."

Bewildered, Angela looked through some of the instructions. "I don't know if—"

"I understand," Carol said. "Between you and me, just feed him and keep him quiet for a while. The incisions are small and most of the sutures are internal. Keep him quiet so he doesn't tear them open. They will all dissolve over time. If you think there's any problem give us a call, but I think he's going to be fine if you just let nature take its course and finish healing him. What he really needs most is rest."

"How long? How long should I keep him in there?"

Carol shrugged. "Maybe a week? Hard to know exactly. I think you'll know when it's time to release him."

Angel tied a heavy old bedspread over the crate to help keep him calm. She drove home relatively slowly, not wanting to give Bardolph a jarring ride or have him fall and rip stitches.

It was cold and clear by the time she got home. She hooked some aluminum ramps on the tailgate and then carefully slid the bedspread-covered crate down onto a bed of straw she'd laid on the ground. She had to go to work to tend bar, so she left the thick bedspread over the crate to help keep him warm. She knew wolves felt safe in dens, so she hoped he would feel that way in his temporary den. There were several big old blankets inside the crate that he could arrange to his liking for bedding.

Before she left for work, she lifted the edge of the bedspread and carefully opened the door just enough to toss in half a raw chicken. Bardolph was pressed up against the back of the crate watching her. His low growl let her know he was not pleased.

Angela talked to him in a calm voice each day when she gave him the chicken. She mostly tried to leave him alone so he wouldn't get stressed or agitated. She wanted to let him rest and heal. Every time she threw in another meal, there was not so much as a scrap left of the previous meal. He managed to do his business in one corner so at least he wasn't lying in it. She would have liked to clean out the crate, but she knew that would be far too dangerous, and besides, once she opened the door enough, he would be out.

After eight days she could tell by how active he was in his crate and the way he snarled at her that he was feeling better and he wanted out. Angela waited two more days and finally decided it was time. She put the ramps back on the tailgate, covered the crate with the old bedspread, and with great effort slid it up the ramps and into the pickup bed.

She didn't really like the idea of releasing a wild wolf by her house. She thought it best if she took him back to where he had been living—near to where the murdered woman had been dumped. He would recognize his territory.

She parked by the side of the road and dropped the tailgate. She pulled the bedspread off and peered in at him in the back of the crate. He growled and snapped at her.

Angela smiled, happy that he had not learned to be unafraid of people.

"I hope you have a good life in your woods," she cooed to him.

Angela climbed up on top of the crate. Holding her gun in one hand, she leaned over to look inside and then carefully opened the latch on the crate with the other.

"Don't you dare attack me now. It cost me a lot of money to get you fixed up. After all that, don't you make me have to shoot you. Run off back to your woods, you hear?"

The wolf remained quiet in the back of the crate. Angela reached out and with a flick of her hand sprang the crate door wide open.

When he still didn't make a move for freedom, she banged a fist on the back of the crate. That was all he needed.

The wolf dashed out of the crate, leaped off the tailgate, and raced away into the woods.

It was a bittersweet moment seeing him stop and turn to look back briefly before loping off into the woods.

Before leaving, Angela flung two raw chickens off into the woods. She hoped he would find the meal and get his belly full.

NINE

"Shit," Brittany said under her breath just before she picked up the tray off the bar.

Angela had just finished putting the four beers on the tray for Brittany to deliver to a table. "What's the problem?"

Brittany gestured with a nod of her head toward the door. "That creepy blind evangelist and the mute are back."

Angela saw that, sure enough, it was the Reverend Baker and his sister Lucy coming in the door. Once she had closed the door, Lucy took her brother's arm to guide him into the room. He swept his white cane from side to side as she led him in.

"Back?" Angela asked. "They've been here before?"

"Yeah. A few weeks ago—when you were off." She stuck a finger through her tangle of teased blond hair to scratch her scalp as she tried to remember. "It was that night we had that first big snow. You remember that big snow?"

"I remember the snow," Angela said, absently, as she watched Lucy lead her brother to a table in the corner on the far side of the restrooms where they both took off their coats. "That was the night I found that woman's body. Kristi Green."

Brittany turned back as it came to her. "Yeah, that's right, the hooker from up the hill. That was the night." She laid a hand on

Angela's forearm. "That must have been horrible, finding her body in the woods like that."

"It was," Angela said.

From what she'd heard on the news, the authorities still hadn't found the woman's killer. Angela knew that it wasn't the guy's first kill. He was a serial killer. That kind of killer was smart, devious, and hard to catch. Sometimes the police never found them.

Angela smiled. Sometimes things happened to them and they simply vanished before the police could ever find them.

One thing was for sure: the killer wasn't going to stop until someone stopped him.

"So the reverend came in late that night?" Angela asked.

"That's right."

Angela guessed that it must have been after the two gave her a ride home. "God's messenger drinks?"

Angela had told Clay Baker and his sister that she tended bar, but she hadn't told them where. It seemed an odd coincidence that they would come into the bar where she worked not long after giving her a ride. Angela didn't like coincidences.

On the other hand, they said they were staying at the Riley Motel. That was just a ways up the hill. If they were looking for a bar, Barry's Place was the closest one.

"They each sucked on a beer for a couple hours," Brittany said. "I think they only bought a couple beers so they could have an excuse to sit there and talk to people."

"Talk to people?"

"You know," Brittany said, popping her gum, "talk to anyone who would listen about life's miseries without Jesus Christ as their savior and how returning to the path of the Lord could bring you eternal happiness, or some shit like that. He bent my ear about God, telling me how I needed to walk the Lord's path."

From what Angela knew about Brittany, she was already a good long way off the path.

36

"He wanted to talk to all the girls about God," Brittany said. "Barry went over and told him that the girls were working and he'd have to talk to them on their own time, after work or something. So then the reverend did the strangest thing."

"What's that?" Angela asked as she washed a glass in the bar sink.

"He and that woman with him left. A little while later they came back with a couple of working girls from up at the Riley." Brittany leaned in with the juicy gossip. "The reverend bought the two hookers drinks just like they were his dates or something. He talked to them for quite a while—trying to 'save' them, I imagine."

"Were they 'saved'?" Angela asked as she dried glasses.

Brittany snorted a laugh. "I don't know, but as long as he was buying drinks they seemed happy to sit there and knock them back while he evangelized. I'd bet you anything they were willing to sit there because they were on his dime."

Angela frowned as she leaned over the bar toward Brittany. "He paid for hookers just so he could preach to them?"

Brittany leaned her head in confidentially and to be heard over the pounding rock music. "From the way they were hanging on his every word, it had to be. Those two weren't going to waste their time just for a drink. They were on the clock. If they can fake an orgasm, they can fake interest in the Lord."

Angela shook her head as she put another glass in the sink. "Wouldn't be the strangest thing I've seen in here."

"That's for sure," Brittany agreed. She turned serious again. "At closing time, they all left. Together."

Angela frowned. "Together?"

"Yeah. I stuck my head out the door to sneak a peek and I saw the girls climb in this big old car with them. They all went back up to the Riley, I guess. For all I know he and the mute paid for a party and all the two girls had to do was sit on his bed and sing hallelujah to him."

Angela watched the pair across the room as she dried another glass. They were too far away and the bar was too dark for her to be able to see them very well, but she could see that Lucy was signing in Reverend Baker's palm.

The rotating ceiling light sent sparkling flecks of light slowly meandering across everything and everyone. It made it harder to see faces. Barry thought the rotating lights gave the place a dreamy, party feel. It was his idea of atmosphere so people would want to stay and buy drinks. That and serving girls in cutoff shorts or miniskirts. The rock music Barry played was so loud it was hard to talk with people without leaning close, which gave men a chance to get in close to women.

"Okay, I have to admit that is pretty weird, but he's just preaching," Angela said. "You said before that there was something creepy about him. What did you mean?"

"I don't know," Brittany finally admitted. She picked up the tray of beers when her customer waved. "For some reason those two just make my skin crawl. Maybe it's those cross tattoos on his cheeks. Maybe it's that mousy, flat-chested woman he has with him. They're a real fucked-up pair, know what I mean?"

Angela arched an eyebrow. "Maybe they're what people are talking about when they say that God works in mysterious ways."

Brittany, holding up the tray with the beers on her upturned palm, was moving her hips to a song she liked. "Could be. He actually tipped me pretty good the last time, so as long as they're buying I guess they can be as mysterious as they damn well please."

As Brittany turned to the room, one of the men sitting close by smiled at her. "You look good moving that fine tail of yours."

"Fuck off," Brittany snapped.

The guy and his buddy laughed. He gave her ass a backhanded smack as she went past. Brittany grinned as she departed with the tray. She liked the attention, and only pretended to object. The guys knew it.

"You know," the guy sitting at the bar said as he munched on a pretzel while turning to Angela, "if you cut those shorts of yours any shorter they won't be able to contain the girls."

She looked up into his eyes. They weren't evil, just bloodshot.

"Thanks for the tip, but I prefer my tips in cash."

The guy and his buddy laughed. They were regulars. They were annoying but harmless. The cutoff shorts Angela wore kept them sitting at the bar, drinking beers. Along with her courier business it helped earn her a good living. Guys like them, though, made her need an occasional hike in the woods.

Guys who were less than harmless made her need other things entirely.

Angela watched Brittany delivering the beers to two couples at a small table. When she was done, Reverend Baker summoned her to his table. She bent close, holding her hair back as she listened to him. Angela assumed they were placing an order. After a brief conversation she returned to the bar.

"What does he want?" Angela asked.

"He wants a couple of beers." She looked over her shoulder briefly and then back at Angela. "And he wanted to know about you."

The hair on the back of Angela's neck stood up.

She set the first beer on the tray. "Me? What did he want to know about me?"

"He wanted to know when you got off. He said he's already talked to all the other girls here about the Lord's path and he would like the chance to talk to you as well. I told him that I thought you knew your path better than anyone I'd ever met. He asked what your path was. I told him, 'Honey, if you ever find out would you please let the rest of us know because we ain't got a clue.'"

Angela smiled. If he gave her any trouble she could knock his cane out of his hands. He'd never be able to catch her.

Still, her inner sixth sense was stirring—the one she had acquired as trouble's child growing up around dangerous men.

TEN

Reverend Baker struck up a conversation with an older man and his wife at a nearby table. Angela could see the couple listening politely. Being so far away and with the music so loud she couldn't hear anything that was being said. It all looked friendly enough, though, with the couple nodding their agreement occasionally. Once they even chuckled at something he said. The reverend didn't look like he was pressing the couple, he looked to be having nothing more than a casual conversation with them. For all Angela knew he might not even be evangelizing.

He and his sister each had two beers and left several hours before last call. They never came over to the bar to say hello to Angela, but he did turn in her direction and wave before going out the door. She was relieved that they didn't want to stay until closing to talk to her. She was tired and just wanted to go home and get some sleep.

It being a weeknight, business slowed down considerably around midnight. By closing time all the other girls had gone home. After last call Barry shooed out the last few customers and locked the door. Angela had put the Reverend Clay Baker and his sister Lucy out of her mind as she cleaned up behind the bar. It was her turn to straighten up after closing. While she swept the floor, Barry went to his little back-room office to close out the night's tally.

After she finished cleaning up, she called out that she was leaving. Barry hurried out with a smile and handed her some folded bills for the previous week's work. As he followed her to the door, he told her to have a good night, and then he locked the door behind her. It was a surprisingly warm night, so Angela simply draped her coat over her arm.

Across the road she could see the jagged tops of the trees in the light of the nearly full moon high overhead. Most of the snow was off them. Barry's Place was at the edge of town, a last stop of sorts, an oasis, for those needing a drink before venturing into the largely uninhabited forested mountains.

Angela's pickup, its gray primer dull in the streetlight, was the only vehicle still in the parking lot. Barry always parked around back. With the above-freezing temps, most of the snow had melted, leaving the parking lot wet and clear of snow except at the edges where it had been piled up by the snowplow that had cleaned the lot.

Just as Angela put the key in to unlock her truck, a car rolled up behind her. She quickly turned the key, unlocking the door. She always carried a Walther P22 in the center console.

She was about to dive in to retrieve the gun when she saw that it was the old, tan Lincoln that Lucy and Reverend Baker drove. She let out a weary sigh, her alarm lowering but her annoyance rising. She wanted to get home and go to bed. She didn't want to have a theological discussion in a chilly parking lot in the wee hours of the morning with a traveling evangelist who had crosses tattooed on his face.

The car sat idling next to her, the cloud of its exhaust rising into the still air. Angela waited patiently for him to open his door so that she could tell him, politely, that she was tired and didn't want to talk to him. She folded her arms and leaned back against her truck. After a moment, both doors of the Lincoln opened.

Reverend Baker stepped out, without his cane, while Lucy emerged from the driver's side.

Frowning, arms still folded, still leaning back against her truck, Angela decided not to wait for his pitch.

"Reverend Baker, before you start telling me about God, I have to stop you. It's late and I'm tired. I don't want to have a discussion tonight."

Out of the corner of her eye, Angela saw Lucy coming around the front of the big, square Lincoln. Whatever expression might have been on her face Angela couldn't see because it was in shadow under the streetlight. Angela realized she had never really gotten a good look at the woman's face.

An odd kind of smile came over Reverend Baker. "I'm not here to discuss God with you, Angela."

"Good."

"You see, God has already chosen you."

Angela frowned. "Sorry, but I didn't raise my hand."

"Oh, but I'm afraid you did."

He lifted his dark glasses and for the first time, in the light from the streetlamp, Angela saw his eyes.

It was like being hit by a bolt of lightning.

They were the eyes of a killer.

In that brief instant, Angela saw the men and women he had murdered. She saw Kristi Green struggling as he wrapped a lamp cord around her neck. The cord was from the Riley Motel room where she thought she was being paid for sex. In her mind's eye, Angela saw him throwing her clothes in the trunk of their car, then dragging her by her ankles into the woods.

Angela saw the young man he had abducted only the day before and intended to torture to death. Clay Baker had an almost uncontrollable hatred of the young man, because he was a male prostitute. But as he was being castrated, the young man had an asthma attack and died. Clay Baker was furious. The man was in the trunk of their car that very moment, waiting to be disposed of.

Looking into his eyes, Angela had instantaneous visions of all the things he had done to all eight women and two men he had murdered over the course of several years. She saw his knife flashing overhead in blind rage as he slammed it down over and over into one woman. Angela saw him carefully, slowly, peeling the skin off a young man gagged and tied to a pole in a dark and grimy railroad yard. She saw him raping a woman after he had beaten her nearly to death.

During it all, his sister was there.

Angela saw that the bite wounds on Kristi Green's breasts were not his. They were Lucy's. He had not broken her ribs. Lucy had.

Angela looked over at the mousy woman standing in the headlights. Her eyes, too, held a world of evil. They were the eyes of a person who enjoyed the slaughter. She was his partner. She lived to see their terror, to be a part of it, even if she let her brother be the one to finally end their lives.

It all came into Angela's mind at once, an instantaneous otherworldly infusion of knowledge. That cascading vision of depravity came to her so fast and hard it hurt.

In that flash of comprehension from what she saw in his eyes, his memories became her memories.

It was the same as it always was when she looked into the eyes of a killer. They were the same kind of visions that always made her bones ache when they flooded into her.

They were the same kind of visions that made her lust to kill these evil men. But this time the visions had her at a distinct disadvantage.

"Ah, I can see the surprise in your eyes," he said with a wicked grin.

"You're not . . ."

"No, I'm not blind. Not at all. You see, I've happened across a few people before who could recognize in my eyes that I've killed people. As I'm sure you can imagine, that became quite awkward and in several instances nearly got me caught.

"As a result I learned that it's in my own best interest to cull that kind of threat from the world before it can harm me. I use the dark glasses of a blind man to hide in plain sight and hunt those like you who can see my secrets in my eyes.

"I have to tell you, I also find it a delightful treat to make that kind suffer. Of course, those others could never have stopped me, but you're different, Angela. I suspect, given the chance, you could.

"That day I took that whore out into the woods, before I could enjoy myself with her, I happened to look up and there, way up through a small open patch in the forest, I saw you coming over the ridge. So I had to kill the whore and leave.

"But I stayed in the area. When I saw you on the road after you found the body and called the police, I knew I had to see who had prevented me from the ecstasy of introducing another whore to Hell. I had to look into your eyes, see if you are one of those who plague me.

"When I offered you a ride I saw that you were. More than that and unlike the others of your kind, I got the feeling that you can see exactly what I've done to those I've killed. Am I right? You see it all, don't you?"

Angela couldn't stop herself from answering. "Yes. I see you for who you really are."

He smiled as he arched an eyebrow. "The devil?"

It suddenly all made sense. They had been out on that desolate road not because they were on their way back from the village of Bradley. Angela had interrupted their kill. That was why they just happened to be there in the area to give her a ride. That was why they had come to the bar.

Angela was angry with herself at how stupid she had been. She knew better than to accept coincidences at face value. But Clay Baker's blind-reverend trick had worked. She had seen what he wanted her to see.

Whatever mistakes she had made were irrelevant now. What Angela needed to do now was kill this bastard.

She turned and yanked open the door of her truck. She dove inside to reach the center console and the gun she kept there. Her fingers grabbed the lid.

As she did, his big fist snatched her by her hair and yanked her back out. Her coat fell from her arms and the keys from her hand.

Angela kicked behind at his shins. He danced away from her strikes. With a firm grip on her hair at the back of her head, he wrenched her around so that her back was to him. She frantically tried to pry his fingers off her hair.

As she did he snaked his left arm in under her arms and around her neck. He released her hair and instead gripped his left arm to put her in a headlock.

Angela struggled, trying every way she could to hit him, scratch him, or gouge out his eyes. She swung with fists and elbows, but with the way he was holding her she couldn't connect effectively. He kept his legs spread so she couldn't kick him or stomp on his feet. She knew he was toying with her.

Then he leaned back, holding her tight up against his chest, lifting her feet from the ground to put more pressure on her neck. As he tightened his arms to compress the carotid arteries in her neck she could feel the world getting fuzzy as the blood supply to her brain was being cut off.

In mere seconds she could feel herself beginning to lose consciousness. Her fingers tingled as the world dimmed.

Her arms flailed, but they flailed with all the limp power of a dream.

In her darkening vision, Angela saw a hand grab her right arm. It was Lucy. She had a syringe in her other hand. She pulled the cap off with her teeth and bent close to put the needle into Angela's arm. She felt the cold sting of something inching up the veins.

With the way Clay Baker had his arm around her neck cutting off not only her circulation, but her air, she couldn't even scream.

She had seen into this monster's mind.

She knew what she was in for.

Sounds faded away as blackness closed in over her.

ELEVEN

Angela became dimly aware of an oppressive darkness. She felt herself being jostled. She was lying on irregular, hard shapes. She had such a horrific headache it made her nauseous.

She blinked, trying to see, but there was only blackness. For a moment, she feared he might have blinded her. He had done that to several of the women before he murdered them. Then she saw a faint glow of red light that finally convinced her that she really was regaining consciousness and she could still see.

But it was an odd, dreamy state of consciousness. Her mouth was dry. Hard as she tried, her tongue couldn't work up any moisture. She was freezing cold. There was something frigid pressed up against her back. Try as she might, she couldn't understand what it was.

After a time of gently rocking back and forth and up and down, it registered that she could only be in the trunk of the big Lincoln. The faint red glow was the light from the taillights leaking out of their housing.

She reached up to push at the trunk lid and found that her wrists were tightly locked together with something hard. She held her wrists up before her face, staring at them as best she could in the faint red glow. Handcuffs. It was handcuffs.

She felt her stomach, breasts, legs, and realized that she was completely naked. She found a small pile of oily rags. She didn't know if her clothes were among them, but she collected all of them together and hugged them to herself as she curled up in a ball, trying to fight off the cold and nausea.

The icy thing behind her kept softly smacking into her back. She struggled to turn around a little, both to get away from it and to try to see what it was.

Once she was on her back, she found that the red glow wasn't enough to reveal what was in the trunk with her. She used her handcuffed hands to reach over to her left. She felt something cold, smooth, and rather firm. She groped along it, feeling for anything that would tell her what it was.

Her fingers glided over a series of bumps. With icy dread she realized it was a human spine. The skin was dead cold.

When the brakes came on, the red glow from the brake lights was considerably brighter and Angela was able to see that the wrists and ankles of the skinny young man had been tightly bound with duct tape.

She realized then that it was the male prostitute Clay Baker had abducted the day before. His body was still there in the trunk with Angela.

When she finally managed to prop herself up on an elbow, she realized that her ankles were taped together with duct tape just like the dead man's. That explained why in her drugged state she couldn't comprehend why her legs weren't following her mental orders. She was pretty sure that if she worked at it she would able to get through the tape, but it would take some time.

Whatever Lucy had injected in her arm had left her groggy and weak. It was a struggle merely to think. Simply moving her arms took great effort.

Summoning her strength, she managed to scoot a little bit away from the dead body. The irregular, hard shape of the trunk floor hurt her back.

The spongy movements of the old Lincoln, the rolling rise and fall, told her that the shocks on the car were shot. Besides her headache, the up and down movements were making her feel seasick. She knew by the dazed way she felt that the drugs were contributing to the nausea. It was taking an effort not to throw up. The last thing she wanted was to have to lie in cold, wet vomit.

Angela thought that maybe when Reverend Killer and Lunatic Lucy eventually opened the trunk she could jump out and run. She realized that was a lousy plan, because even if she could get the duct tape off her ankles, when they eventually opened the trunk it would take a slow, clumsy effort to climb out, and even if she was able to get out she didn't think she had enough strength in her legs to run. She was so dizzy she wasn't even convinced she would be able to stand.

Angela wondered what had been in that syringe. By her uncoordinated thinking and floundering attempts to move she knew it had to be something powerful. Clay Baker said that his sister had once worked in a hospital. She would have had access to drugs and syringes.

These two had done this before. They were experienced. They knew what to do to make sure their victims didn't have a chance to fight back or escape.

Angela hated drugs. Drugs had robbed her of her childhood. They had robbed her of a real mother. They had brought danger and pain into her world. After everything she'd seen, she would never take drugs. She didn't even drink.

But now these two depraved psychos had drugged her.

TWELVE

Angela didn't know how long they drove, but she guessed it must have been about an hour. In the beginning they stopped at lights or stop signs, but once they started moving at a steady pace she knew they had left Milford Falls. She had no clue where they could be taking her, but it seemed obvious they were taking her out into the countryside. When Reverend Baker was done with her, he would dump her body in the woods like he had done with the murdered woman Angela had found.

She could tell that the drugs had begun wearing off a little, because her thoughts weren't quite so fragmented. As they drove on into the night, Angela worked at the duct tape on her ankles. She had to scoot farther away from the body behind her so that she had more room to work. The effort took time, and at first she didn't know that in the dark she could do it. But bit by bit she tore through all the layers and was finally able to pull off the thick mass of duct tape. She felt a flush of triumph at the small victory.

As they drove for a while through what she knew had to be the countryside she picked through the rags trying to find her clothes. In the dark, pitching trunk, she found her panties. Putting them on was the second small victory. Before she could find any more of her clothes, the car slowed. It crept along the road briefly, and then turned abruptly and stopped. The transmission clanked and the car reversed direction, backing off the road. As they bounced through the dip of a shallow ditch, it banged Angela's head against the trunk lid.

The engine shut off. Angela listened, trying to hear what was going on. Almost immediately she heard the doors open and then slam shut.

She urgently turned herself in the shallow space and drew her knees up to her chest as best she could, getting ready for when they opened the trunk. Her heart pounded in her ears. She swallowed back against the fear rising in her throat.

This might be her only chance—her last chance. She reached up and behind with her handcuffed hands and grabbed hold of metal around the trunk's hinge. She had learned long ago, growing up at her mother's trailer, that when dealing with psychos you couldn't hesitate to take any opportunity that presented itself to escape.

The trunk lid suddenly sprang up. In the moonlight she could see a tall, dark shape, and a short one.

The taller shape bent down. With all of her strength, with her hands braced on the metal framework above her head, Angela kicked her feet out at the head of the dark shape leaning in toward her. She felt her heels connect. He cried out in surprise and pain as he stumbled back.

Angela snatched up a jack handle she had found during the long ride. Armed with the metal bar, she managed to climb out of the trunk. With all her strength she swung at him. His hands covered his face, so his arms blocked the blow she had hoped to land against his head. Even so, it was clear by the way he cried out how much it hurt when the metal bar hit bone.

"Fucking little bitch!" he screamed.

He immediately reached for her. Angela swung, this time connecting with his outstretched hand.

He flinched back, bending over holding his hand. He let out an angry howl of pain. Angela had no strength left. She was moving on sheer force of will fueled by fear. She hoped that if she could stop him for long enough she could run and hide. They might never find her if she hid in the dark woods. She just needed one more blow to stagger him back far enough so he couldn't reach out and grab her when she made her escape.

As Angela took another mighty swing, he backed away just in time to avoid her landing another blow.

As the heavy jack handle swung around in the follow-through, Lucy suddenly flew out of the darkness and slammed into Angela from the side. Angela crashed to the ground with Lucy on top of her.

Clay Baker's boot immediately came down on the back of her neck, pressing her face into the ground. Lucy twisted Angela's arm with the jack handle behind her and with a knee in the small of her back helped her brother pin Angela down. The small but surprisingly strong woman wrenched the metal bar from Angela's hand and tossed it away out of reach.

Lucy used her teeth to pull the cap off a syringe and used her free hand to jam the needle in Angela's bottom and shove the plunger home.

Angela felt the hot sting of all the liquid tearing into the muscle all at once.

With one boot already on her neck, Clay Baker stepped up and placed the other on her back. He balanced on top of her to keep her down. She had trouble drawing a breath. It had been a valiant effort. She had struck several blows to the monster, but in the end, Angela was on the ground, struggling just to breathe under the weight of both of them.

She could feel herself tingling as the drugs moved through her bloodstream. Her mind grew numb as she struggled to remain conscious. It seemed not to matter anymore. In mere moments she was incapacitated. Clay Baker stepped down off her. Lucy brushed herself off as she got back up on her feet.

Angela lay on the ground, the world slowly spinning and tipping every which way around her. She tried to stand. Her legs folded. She realized she couldn't even remember how to stand.

Clay Baker kicked her in the ribs, knocking her back down. "You stupid fucking little bitch!" His scream echoed back from the still, moonlit forest. "You goddamn whore!"

She could feel hot drops of blood from his bleeding nose falling like fat drops of rain on her back. He leaned down toward her, cursing at her in a blind rage.

Angela couldn't even feel satisfaction at having hurt him. She could hardly feel anything. She scarcely knew where she was anymore.

Clay Baker grabbed her by the hair and hauled her to her feet. He gritted his teeth as he put his bloody face close to hers.

"I don't think you can begin to imagine what we're going to do to you." He pointed at his broken nose. "You think this hurts? We're going to show you what hurt really is. This is nothing compared to what you're going to feel."

He pulled Angela from her feet and dragged her across the small opening in the forest until he reached an area of deadfalls. He hauled her limp body beyond the half dozen tangled logs on the ground and the splintered stumps to a tree that was still standing. He pushed her up against the trunk.

"Hold her," he told his sister.

Lucy put a hand under each breast and pushed against Angela's ribs to hold her back against the rough tree bark. He grabbed her handcuffed wrists and grunted with the effort as he lifted her up until he was able to hook the cuffs over a limb.

The limb of the tree had been cut recently. As Angela hung from that limb she could see out over the small opening in the forest. The spot, clear of tress, lit by the nearly full moon high overhead, looked familiar.

With dread, she remembered then, what was familiar about the spot. This was where she had found the wolf feeding on the corpse of Kristi Green.

Angela remembered the visions she'd had looking into his eyes. He had taken Kristi Green out of the trunk and dragged her to this place. This was where he had started to torture the terrified woman. But then he had spotted Angela hiking up on the ridge. In a hasty act of self-preservation, he had stabbed her in the chest at least a dozen times—quick violent punches—and then left her lifeless body there on the ground while he and Lucy escaped.

After leaving, they had driven around the area, going up and down the road a few times. After the police and crime scene people had arrived, he drove down the road and found Angela walking home through the snowstorm. Angela had foolishly thought it was a lucky break to get a ride home.

"Get the bag out of the car," Baker growled at his sister.

She hesitated and then signed something. He went ballistic.

"What! How could you be that stupid! How could you leave our tools at the motel!"

Lucy withered under his screaming fit. She backed away a step, clearly afraid he would hit her. Her fear was well founded. He punched her once, then a moment later hit her again.

After a few minutes he started to calm down. She signed, apparently offering to drive back to the motel and get what she had forgotten.

"No," he finally said after glaring at Angela for a time. "No, I'll go get them. I want to bandage up my nose. I'll get the bag."

Lucy hung her head, not wanting to look up at him.

He stepped close to Angela, hate twisting the crosses tattooed on his cheeks. "We have a bag of special tools. Things we use to make whores like you suffer. I can't wait to get started in on you." He smiled. "While I'm gone, I'll let Lucy introduce you to your new world of pain. Lucy really hates cheap godless whores like you. You'll see."

Angela wanted to spit in his bloody face, but she couldn't seem to summon the strength or the spit.

He turned to Lucy. "You can get started on her while I go get cleaned up and get our tools."

As he hurried back to the car, Lucy finally looked up at Angela and smiled. Her smile was just as wicked as her brother's.

THIRTEEN

After her brother had left, Lucy foraged around on the moonlit forest floor among the deadfall for a time, picking up limbs and then discarding them as unsatisfactory. She at last found one that seemed to satisfy her. She stepped on the end and broke off the extra until she had something just a little longer than a baseball bat. She whacked it against a fallen tree trunk, then took a few test swings. She seemed satisfied.

Angela contorted herself as she hung by the handcuffs, trying to get them loose from the limb. With her arms stretched over her head and the handcuffs hooked over the stump of the limb, she couldn't get herself free. She looked up and saw branches that had been sawed off the limb, leaving stubs that kept the cuffs from sliding off.

Angela's weight was largely hanging in the handcuffs. She had to stretch up on her tiptoes to take weight off her wrists and catch her breath. She could feel warm blood running down her arms from where the cuffs cut into her flesh.

Lucy returned and without ceremony took an experimental swing, landing a blow on the side of Angela's ribs. She gasped at the shock of sudden, brutal pain.

Lucy stepped close. Leaning in, she inspected her handiwork. She ran her small fingers over the spot where she had landed the blow, feeling the torn skin, testing if she'd broken a rib.

Then she put her mouth on the side of Angela's left breast and bit down as hard as she could.

Despite being in a dazed mental fog, Angela screamed. Tears of agony ran down her cheeks as she twisted from side to side trying to get away from the viselike grip of Lucy's teeth. The pain was stunning. It felt like Lucy was taking a big bite of flesh out of her.

When she finally let go, Angela couldn't hold herself up on her toes. She hung in the handcuffs, panting from the pain, unable to comfort the bite wound. Lucy immediately swung her club, slamming it into Angela's right side. It hit just below the ribs. Before she could get her breath, Lucy bit down in a new spot on Angela's left breast.

All Angela could think of was how much she wanted the pain to stop.

Lucy straightened and showed Angela a bloody smile. Lucy was a psychopath. Along with her psycho brother they were an incredibly dangerous pair. They had tortured and murdered innocent people in the name of spreading the word of God.

Lucy swung again, landing a blow on Angela's ribs on the other side. It made a sickening sound. The eye-watering pain made Angela dance on her toes, trying to find a way to make it stop hurting.

In that instant the pain crossed over to rage.

Angela strained with her arm muscles to curl up, drew in her legs, and with all her strength suddenly slammed both feet into the center of Lucy's chest.

Angela had strong legs. The powerful blow knocked the wind from Lucy's lungs and violently threw her back.

As the small woman was flung back, her body twisted as she stumbled and fell. She landed on one of the standing spearlike splinters rising up from the stump of a deadfall.

Still angry, Angela managed to bounce herself in the handcuffs enough that they popped off the limb.

Finally free, she snatched up the club that Lucy had used on her. Fearing to lose the advantage, she ran around the stump, intending to use the heavy club on Lucy. She saw, then, that there was no urgency.

Lucy had fallen forward onto the large spike of wood. It had gone in through her soft upper belly just under the bottom of her rib cage. She was so deeply impaled she couldn't pull herself off. The shock of it had stunned her. She scraped at base of the stump with her toes, trying to lift herself off, but the wooden spike was in so deep that it was clearly hopeless.

Lucy's wide eyes stared at Angela pleading for help. Her hands clawed the air as if she was trying to find something to pull herself off the jagged spear of wood.

Her mouth opened wide, trying to scream. Only a gurgling, wet cry came forth.

And then blood started oozing up into her mouth. It ran out and poured off her chin. Her eyes blinked as she started choking, coughing, and gagging, trying to get a breath as her lungs filled with blood.

Angela, still panting with rage, stepped closer. She could have used the club to bash in Lucy's skull and end the woman's misery. But Angela didn't want the misery to end. How many people had this woman hurt? How much misery had she inflicted? How many victims had she tortured before her brother killed them?

Angela left the struggling woman drowning in her own blood and staggered away, intent on escaping. The effort had taken everything out of her. The adrenaline had overpowered the drugs briefly. Now she was sinking back into a stupor.

As she tried to take a step she collapsed onto her side.

The bleeding bite wounds throbbed so painfully that even in the drug haze Angela could hardly take it. She clawed at the ground, scooping up handfuls of snow that hadn't yet melted. With trembling fingers she pressed the snow to the bite wounds on her breasts. The freezing snow hurt, but it helped numb the greater hurt of the bites. She put snow on the painful wound on her ribs. She didn't know if they were broken or not.

As she lay in the bed of dried leaves panting, watching Lucy's struggles slow, Angela felt herself slipping away into unconsciousness.

FOURTEEN

The cold and icy snow against her flesh brought Angela awake. She didn't know how long she had lain in the snow. It might have been that the cold had to a degree overcome the effects of the drugs, but for whatever reason she was starting to be able to form coherent thoughts. Angela realized that if she lay there on the ground she was going to die. Even if she didn't die of exposure, Clay Baker was going to come back and find her there. When he did, he would kill her.

Angela forced herself to her feet. She couldn't feel her toes. Her fingers were numb, too. She needed to get away before he came back. She needed to escape, or hide, or something. She just knew that she had to move if she wanted to live, and she desperately wanted to live.

In the moonlight she could see that Lucy was dead. A little bit of blood still dripped from her chin, so Angela knew the woman couldn't have been dead for long.

Angela looked around. She remembered the place from the day she had hiked in. She remembered where the dead woman had been. She could go back the way she had come when she hiked in.

She decided that naked, in the dark, she would not make it far. The fastest way out or to get help would be the road.

She forced herself to start moving down toward the road. It was a struggle to put one foot in front of the other. She was so cold all she could think about was getting warm again. She staggered along and soon saw the moonlight on the ribbon of road off through the trees. That gave her a bit of hope and she moved more quickly. If Clay Baker came back and found her she was a dead woman.

Not quite to the road yet, she stopped in the place where the big Lincoln had pulled in off the road so she could listen for cars. She didn't want to walk out on the road and be in the open just as he came driving up. She decided that if she couldn't hear any cars, she would walk along near the ditch, and if she saw car lights or heard his car coming she would dart into the woods and hide.

As she considered that idea, she realized that if it wasn't Clay Baker coming back and it was just someone driving down the road, she would lose the chance to stop them for help. She would lose her chance to get into a warm car. She very well might lose her chance to live.

She was so tired she just wanted to lie down and rest, but she knew that if she did that she would never get up. Instead, she stood while she rested, hands on her knees, letting her head hang for a moment. As she stood panting from both terror and the effort of moving with the cold and the drugs in her system, she saw moonlight reflect off something.

Frowning, she stared for a moment, trying to figure out what it was. She realized it had square corners.

Angela finally squatted down and picked it up out of the tire track in the forest debris.

It was a phone.

The cheap phone was bent a little and the lower right corner of the glass was cracked. Clay Baker must have dropped his phone when he went back to his car. When he drove away he had run over it, breaking the glass.

Angela pressed the button and was stunned to see the screen light up. It wasn't locked. It had over half its battery life left.

Hope shot through her in a flash of hot excitement.

She could call 911 and get help. They would come. She would be safe.

She hit the button for the phone. A number pad came up.

Angela pressed the 9 to call 911. Nothing happened. She pressed all the other numbers and they all worked. But the severe crack going right across the 9 kept it from working.

Angela wanted to scream up at the sky for fate bringing her so close to salvation, yet leaving her so far away.

She reminded herself that she didn't believe in fate. She believed in herself. She racked her drug-hazed brain trying to think of something.

Deputy Nolan's number popped into her head.

She had seen that number on his card. She remembered it because of the repeating 2s. Hoping against hope, she hit the first number. The phone beeped and put the number up on the screen. Shaking with excitement, she dialed the second number and then the third. They worked. She dialed the 2s and they all worked.

Giddy with excitement she put the phone up to her ear, listening to it ring. The call rang and then went to a recording. Angela growled in frustration. She dialed it again, and again got voice mail. She left messages, telling him it was Angela Constantine and she needed help. She told him where she was.

Her moment of relief faded. She knew it could be hours before he woke up and got the messages. Some people didn't even look at their messages until later in the day.

She would be dead by then.

In frustration she dialed the number over and over. Listening to it ring, and then go to voice mail. She kept dialing, furious that he wasn't answering.

"Who the hell is this!" an irate voice suddenly said.

Angela blinked. "It's Angela."

"What? Who the hell are you and why do you keep calling me?"

He was clearly angry. She remembered his angry eyes when he looked at her.

"It's Angela Constantine."

"Who?"

"Trouble's child."

There was silence for a moment. "Trouble's child? You mean the girl who found that body? That Angela Constantine?"

"Yes!" she said, tears in her voice. "Help me! Please, I need help. He's going to kill me."

"Are you drunk? You sound drunk."

"They abducted me. They drugged me. I'm sorry I can't talk very good. They stuck me with a needle and drugged me."

"Who drugged you?"

"Reverend Baker."

"Who the hell is Reverend Baker and why in the world would a reverend drug you?"

"He's the one!" Angela cried into the phone as she sank to her knees. "He's the one who murdered that woman—Kristi Green—and dumped her in the woods! He's a psychopath. He's going to be back soon. He's going to murder me. Please, I need help."

"Why didn't you call 911?"

"I can't, goddamn it!" she screamed. "The phone's broken! The nine doesn't work! I remembered your number."

Angela froze when she heard a car. As it sailed past she saw that it was a pickup, not Reverend Baker's car.

Phone to her ear, Angela staggered back into the woods. She had to hide.

"Where are you now?" Deputy Nolan asked.

"The woods," Angela mumbled.

"That doesn't tell me anything. What woods? Where?"

Her head was spinning. The whole forest was spinning.

"The woods where he left the body. He took my clothes. I'm freezing to death. He'll be back any second. He's going to find me and kill me."

"All right, you stay on the phone. I'm going to get help."

Angela started crying with relief. Her fingers were so numb the phone fell to the ground. She staggered a few steps, knowing that she needed to run and hide. She couldn't take another step.

Her head spun. She felt sure she was going to throw up. As blackness overwhelmed her, she collapsed to the ground.

FIFTEEN

Angela was jolted awake when light and sound suddenly flooded through the woods. The engine and headlights cut off and she heard a car door open and then slam shut.

"Lucy!" he called out. "I'm back!"

Angela blinked, trying to wake up enough to think what to do. She had to get away. She had to run and hide.

She heard another car door open as he got something out of the backseat. By the metallic rattle, she assumed it could only be his bag of torture tools. When he found her, he would use those things on her. He would see his sister dead, and then he would find Angela.

Angela forced herself to her feet. If she didn't get away, she was going to die. Sheer willpower made her move. Sheer terror of him catching her made her put one foot in front of the other. He must have heard the noise she was making as she stumbled through the forest, because she could hear his footsteps rushing in her direction.

Angela's legs gave out and she fell on her face not far from Lucy's impaled body.

Clay Baker saw them both at the same time. The canvas bag he was holding hit the ground with a metallic clank.

"What have you done? What have you done!" he screamed. "What the fuck have you done!"

"I killed the bitch," Angela said. "And now I'm going to kill you."

She rose up with the metal jack handle that was on the ground where she had fallen. As he came for her she started swinging. She could hear the bar whistling through the air as she swung at his head. She connected with his forearm when he thrust it up to protect his face. By the sound, she broke the bone.

Clay Baker staggered back, howling in pain and rage.

Angela kept swinging as she advanced. She wanted more than anything in the world to kill this monster. She wanted him dead. She swung with all her might. She swung with everything she had.

He caught the metal jack handle in his fist.

The crosses tattooed on Clay Baker's cheeks distorted when he grinned at her in the moonlight. His broken left arm hung down. He held the jack handle in his fist with more power than she had any chance to overcome. The metal bar might as well have been stuck in stone.

"Now you die," he said in a terrifyingly soft voice.

He ripped the jack handle from her hands and threw it off into the woods. She heard it thunk against a tree trunk.

Angela turned and started to run, but it felt like her legs were trying to run through knee-deep mud. She knew she wouldn't be able to run fast enough to get away from him, but driven by sheer terror all she could do was run. The drugs were weighing her down, but at the same time a flood of adrenaline was lifting her up and helping her run.

Over her shoulder Angela saw him bend down and open the canvas bag. When he stood, she could see the moonlight reflect off the blade of a big knife.

Angela ran faster. At least, in her mind, she was running faster. But he wasn't running. Taking big strides, he had no difficulty closing the distance to her.

When he caught up with her, he shoved her from behind, trying to push her down. Angela staggered forward and managed to stay on her feet. She spun around to fend him off.

He was still grinning. "First, I'm going to stick you good. Then I'm going to cut you open and let your guts spill out on the ground."

He smiled as he showed her the knife in his big fist. Angela was spent. She knew she had no strength left to fight off a knife-wielding killer.

Knife high overhead, he lunged forward to stab her.

In the moonlight she saw the blade flashing down toward her.

All of a sudden, Angela saw teeth come out of nowhere. The big black wolf crashed into Clay Baker, clamping its jaws onto his arm.

As he tumbled back to the ground, the wolf madly shook the arm, ripping flesh from bone. The reverend screamed, trying to bat the wolf away with his broken arm. But the wolf had a death grip on the arm. He shook it so hard it flopped Clay Baker's body across the ground like a rag doll. He shrieked as the wolf shook violently, twisted, and yanked.

As the reverend tried to pull the mangled arm back from the jaws, Angela could see white bone down through torn flesh. Baker was still shrieking at the top of his lungs.

Angela tried to stand and couldn't, so she crawled on her hands and knees, groping around on the ground for the knife he had dropped.

Clay Baker finally managed to get his arm out of the wolf's jaws, and started kicking frantically to keep the animal off him. As the wolf circled, the reverend turned himself on his back and kicked at it.

When he kicked again, the wolf snatched the ankle in its teeth and started wildly twisting and shaking. Clay Baker screamed and kicked with his other foot. He landed a powerful kick on the animal's rib cage. The wolf yelped in pain as the blow sent it rolling through the snow.

On her knees, the knife held in both fists, Angela lifted her arms high over her head. His eyes went wide as he saw what was coming. Angela slammed the blade down through the center of Clay Baker's face, where the bones were most fragile.

His legs fell limp to the ground. She let go of the knife. Only the handle and an inch of blade stood proud of the bloody face. He had died in an instant. She wished she could have made him suffer, but she would take simply killing the monster.

In the sudden silence, with both of the killers dead, Angela's strength was exhausted. She crawled a short distance away and fell over into a thick bed of leaves.

As hard as she tried, she couldn't keep the darkness from taking her. She knew that, this time, she would never wake. This time, death would finally have her.

SIXTEEN

Angela felt hands on her shoulders. She struggled, pushing with her heels, trying to back away from the grip of the killer.

"Easy," a voice said. "You're safe now."

She didn't know how the monster was still alive, but somehow he was and now he was grabbing her.

"Easy. It's all right, Angela. Calm down. You're safe."

Angela blinked. It was the stern face of Deputy Nolan. He was down on one knee beside her.

She half laughed, half cried in relief.

He straightened and took off his black leather jacket, then swung the coat around her bare shoulders and pulled it together over the front of her.

He had driven his patrol car right up past the Lincoln and into the clearing. The lights from the car lit up the scene.

"They drugged me. They were going to kill me," she said, "like they killed that other girl in this same place. Kristi Green. They wanted to kill me here as revenge for interrupting them before."

He was nodding as he unlocked the handcuffs. "It's all right now. You're safe now."

Angela could hear sirens wailing in the distance.

"I killed the bastard," she said.

He looked back over his shoulder. "Killed him dead," he confirmed. "He looks pretty badly torn up, too."

"It was a wolf that saved me. Just as he was about to stab me to death, the wolf came out of nowhere and took him down. He dropped the knife. I grabbed it. As he was fighting off the wolf, I stabbed him with it.

"After that . . . I don't know what happened after that."

Deputy Nolan frowned down at her. "Well, without any clothes and as cold as it is you should have died of exposure out here."

Angela shook her head. "I don't understand why I didn't."

The deputy gave her an odd look. "When I ran in here I had my gun drawn. In the headlights I saw those eyes shining at me from over the top of you. It was a wolf."

"What? He was still here?"

"He sure was. He was laying down, pressed up tight against you. If I didn't know better, I'd say he was trying to keep you warm. Craziest thing I ever saw."

"Bardolph. That's his name. He was keeping me warm?"

Deputy Nolan nodded. "Damnedest thing. When I first pulled in here and saw him I almost shot at him, but I decided not to for fear I might hit you. He just looked up at me a moment, then he ran off."

"Yeah," Angela said, "you pull your first shot low and to the right."

He puzzled at her briefly. "Come on, let me help you up. I need to get you to my car where it's warm."

He finally gave up trying to help her walk and instead scooped her up in his arms. He carried her to his car and gently placed her in the front seat where the heater could blow on her. His patrol car was toasty warm inside. Even so, she couldn't stop her teeth from chattering. With shaking fingers she clutched his warm coat tight around herself.

"I think some of my clothes might be in the trunk of his Lincoln. There's another of their victims in there as well—the body of a young man."

He shook his head at the news. "Okay, let me go see if I can find you some clothes, then you're going to have to explain all this to me."

Angela nodded, not entirely sure how she could explain it all.

Deputy Nolan, hand on the window frame of the open door, paused and leaned back in. "Anthony."

Angela frowned up at him. "What?"

"You asked my first name before. It's Anthony."

Angela finally smiled. "Thank you for coming to help me, Anthony."

For the first time she saw him smile, too. It wasn't a big grin, but it was a smile. She could tell he was a man who didn't smile often. He probably thought it made him look weak.

"Sit tight. I'll see if I can find your clothes," he said before shutting the door of his patrol car.

Angela sat with her knees pulled up to her chest, huddled inside his warm leather coat.

She looked out the front window and saw eyes shining back from the woods. Bardolph was sitting on his haunches, watching her from back in the woods.

She smiled out at the wolf and lifted her hand so he would know she saw him.

He turned then and trotted off into the dark forest.

She looked over and saw Deputy Anthony Nolan coming with her clothes. Clay Baker was dead. Lucy Baker was dead. Angela was alive. Bardolph, the fierce wolf, was safe and free.

But Angela had learned a hard lesson. It was illegal to carry a gun and having it in her truck wasn't close enough to always save her. From now on she was going to carry a knife.

A serious knife.

AVAILABLE NOW

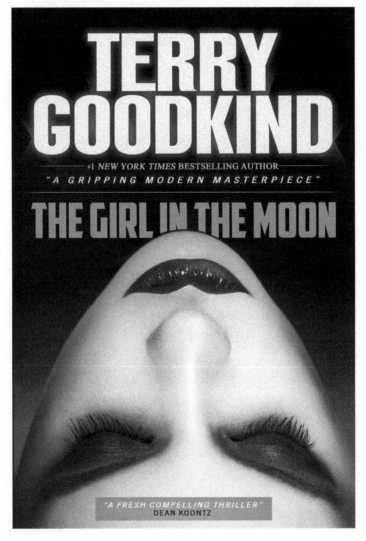

In his newest heart-pounding novel, #1 *New York Times*
bestselling author Terry Goodkind introduces the world
to his most unforgettable and deadly character yet.

Angela Constantine is . . . *The Girl in the Moon.*

ONE

When Angela glanced up and saw him out in the parking lot beyond the neon beer sign hung in the bar's small front window, her first thought was to wonder if this was the night she was going to die.

The unexpected storm of emotion drove other thoughts from her mind. She wondered if this might be why she had just that morning changed the color of her hair from a bright violet to platinum blond that down the length gradually changed to pale pink that became darker until it was a vivid red at the tips, as if her hair had been dipped in blood. Signs sometimes came to her in such subtle ways.

Under the lone streetlight, she could see that the man was wearing a hooded, camo rain slicker. He paused momentarily to glance around in the drizzly darkness. The rain slicker gave him a hulking appearance. His gaze went from the bar's sign, BARRY'S PLACE, to the neon beer sign, and then to the door.

She suspected he wanted a drink in the hopes of keeping a high from fading as the distance of days dulled the rapture.

They sometimes did that.

His indecision was brief. When he came through the doorway, his dark shape made it seem as if he were dragging the night in with him.

Seeing him standing in the dim light inside as he paused to glance around at the patrons, Angela felt a sickening mix of hot revulsion and icy fear laced with a heady rush of lust. She let the feeling wash over her, euphoric that she could feel something, even this.

It had been too long since she had felt anything.

Her hand with the towel slowed to a stop at drying a glass as she waited to see how long it would take him to notice her—her fear hoping he didn't, her inner need hoping he did.

That dark, awakening desire won out.

Out of the corner of her eye she watched as he started toward the bar. Slowly rotating flecks of colored light from the ceiling fixture played over his camouflaged form, almost making him look like part of the room. Behind him, out beyond the window, the headlights of a passing car illuminated the murky drizzle. Fog was moving in. It was going to be a nasty night to be out in the mountains.

Other than a couple of older local men down at the end of the bar arguing baseball, and four Mexicans she had never seen before at a table near the front chattering in Spanish over their beers, the bar was empty. Barry, the bar's owner, was in back checking stock and paperwork.

The man pushed his hood back as his gaze took in her platinum-blond hair tipped in red, her black fingernail polish, the row of rings piercing the back of her right ear, the glitter on her dark eye shadow, and her bare midriff. As he hoisted himself up on a stool, his gaze played over her low-rise, cutoff shorts and down the length of her long legs to the laced brown suede boots that came up almost to her knees.

Barry, the owner, liked her to wear cutoff shorts because it brought in men and kept them longer to buy more drinks. It made her better tips as well. When she'd cut the legs as short as possible, she left the pockets so she would have a place to put her tips. They hung down below the frayed bottoms of the legs. But, with the late hour, there weren't many customers left or tips to be had.

And then, for a fleeting second when he lifted his face and looked up into her eyes, she stopped breathing.

In that instant, looking into his dark, wide-set eyes, she saw everything. Every horrific detail. The flood of it all was momentarily overwhelming. She thought her knees might buckle.

Angela finally leaned in on the bar to steady herself and so that she could be heard over the pounding beat of the rock music. "What can I get you?"

"A beer," he called back over the music.

He was youngish although older than her, maybe in his late twenties, with shaggy hair and scraggly stubble on his doughy face. She noted that he looked strong. When he took off his dripping wet slicker and tossed it over the next stool she saw that she had underestimated how powerfully he was built—not bodybuilder strong, but sloppy, stocky strong, the kind of man who didn't know his own strength until it was too late.

To others his features might appear ordinary, but Angela now knew for certain that this man was anything but ordinary.

After she drew the beer, she set it on the bar in front of him. She licked foam that had run over the glass off the back of her hand and then from her red lipstick as she glanced past him to the clock on the wood-paneled wall to the right. It was less than an hour to closing. Not much time. She pulled a bowl of corn chips from under the counter and set it beside his beer.

"Thanks," he said as he took a chip.

She turned back to drying glasses, but not so far as to let him think she was spurning his obvious interest in her. "If you want more just ask," she said without looking at him, giving him the opportunity to stare down the length of her body.

He took a long drink along with the long look and then made a satisfied sound. "That hits the spot."

"You live in the area?" she asked, looking back over her shoulder.

"Not really."

She turned toward him. "What does that mean?"

He shrugged. "I've been staying just up the road at the Riley Motel." He deliberately glanced down at her legs. "But I may stay for a while longer, find some work."

The Riley Motel wasn't the kind of place tourists visiting the upper reaches of the Appalachian Mountains or the Finger Lakes region would likely stay. The Riley was used mostly by the hour by prostitutes and by the week by transients.

"Oh yeah? What kind of work? What do you do?"

He shrugged. "Whatever needs doing that pays the bills."

Angela poured a shot and set it down in front of him. "On me— for a first-time new customer who may be staying for a while."

He made an appreciative face and tossed back the shot. As he plunked the shot glass down on the bar, his gaze again drifted down the length of her.

"Kind of a dumpy place for a girl like you."

"It pays the bills." She had to deliberately slow her breathing. "What's your name?"

He held her gaze as he took another corn chip. "Owen."

She had trouble looking away from his eyes and all that they told her.

"And yours?"

"Angela. My grandparents were Italian. Angela means 'angel' in Italian." With a flick of her head, she tossed a disorderly shock of red-tipped hair back over her shoulder. "My mother named me Angela because when she was pregnant with me my grandmother said that God was sending her a little angel."

Angela's grandfather told her once that the meaning of the name Angel was "messenger from God," and that while the messenger had come, Angela's mother clearly hadn't gotten the message.

Owen's gaze moved from her eyes to the tattoo across her throat. "Is that some kind of joke?"

Angela flashed him a cryptic smile. "Maybe sometime you'll have the opportunity to answer that question yourself."

His expression darkened. "You fucking with me?"

She leaned in on an elbow so no one else would hear over the music and looked at him from under her brow. "Believe me, Owen, if I ever start fucking with you, you'll know it."

He didn't quite know what to make of her answer, so he drank the rest of the beer. It was obvious that he was more interested in leering at her legs than trying to figure out what she'd meant.

Rather than wait for him to order another as he set down the empty glass, she set a fresh beer in front of him. She took the empty away and put it in the bar sink.

"Attentive little thing, aren't you?"

She put on a flirty smile. "Someone needs to take care of a man like you," she said as she poured another shot and dropped it in the beer.

He returned a grin and drank it all down, almost as if showing off.

"Maybe," he said as he set the glass down and wiped his mouth with the back of his hand, "you could take even better care of me? What do you say?"

Her smile turned empty. "Sorry. You're not my type."

"What the fuck does that mean?"

She placed both hands wide on the edge of the bar as she leaned in and spoke intimately. "I like dangerous guys who take what they want and don't take no for an answer. Know what I mean?"

He frowned. "No. What do you mean?"

She paused for only an instant to invent a story. "I started going with my last boyfriend after he killed a guy."

"Killed a guy? Straight-up killed him?"

"Well," she drawled, "not like murdered him for the rush of doing it. I don't think he had the balls for that. He killed the guy in a fight." She gestured to the door. "Some drunk jumped him out in the parking lot when he left here. He broke the guy's neck." She winked as her smile returned. "Turned me on no end, know what I mean?"

"Sounds like a badass."

"He was." She shrugged as she pulled back. "That's my kind of man. You don't have what it takes."

He weighed her words as he studied her face, her wild shock of red-tipped hair, the tattoo across her throat, the piercings. "I have my rough side."

Angela huffed a laugh to dismiss his claim before turning to reach in and replace the whiskey bottle on a shelf in front of the smoked mirror on the back wall.

In the mirror she could see him looking at her ass.

She knew what he was thinking.

In a million years he would never be able to guess what she was thinking.

CPSIA information can be obtained
at www.ICGtesting.com
Printed in the USA
LVHW032111310519
619765LV00001B/77/P

9 781510 748026